RUSS THOMPSON

LETTERZ

Finding Forward Books

Published by Finding Forward Books
P.O. Box 8182, Long Beach, CA 90808
www.findingforwardbooks.com

Editing by Laura Perkins. Series concept by
Pam Sheppard. Text set in Open Dyslexic Mono.

LCCN: 2023916708
ISBN: 979-8-9890657-0-7 (print)
ISBN: 979-8-9890657-1-4 (ebook)
FILE: FF009-26E-2025-03-08

Summary: A teen struggling with dyslexia
learns to adapt and succeed in high school.

BISAC Subject Codes: YOUNG ADULT FICTION /
School and Education / General | YOUNG ADULT
FICTION / Social Themes / Emotions and
Feelings | YOUNG ADULT FICTION / Social
Themes / Depression

Lexile readability measure: HL420L

For Betty Jean,

our kids,

and grandkids.

CONTENTS

1	Grab It	1
2	Do You Think?	6
3	Same Thing	9
4	Any Other	16
5	Over	23
6	Now They Know	28
7	Give It	36
8	Believe Her	42
9	Changed Today	50
10	Catch Up	54
11	But I'm Not	59
12	Head Down	64
13	Chance Now	69
14	Real Reason	73
15	Why Do I?	79
16	Feel Close	85
17	If They Can	91
18	I Was	95

19   Finally   99

20   Letters   103

Acknowledgments   108

About the Author   110

Finding Forward Books   111

Additional Titles   112

1 GRABIT

EDISON HIGH. I walk through the front gate.

It's the first day of school.

It's my second year of tenth grade.

I hate this place.

The bell rings. I go to World History and sit in the back.

Alex and Leon are already there. They failed it last year, too.

The name on the board says Mr. Hanzen.

He's an old guy with bushy

eyebrows and a frown on his face.

He comes to the front and clicks on his laptop.

A PowerPoint shows on the screen.

I read the title to myself. It says Clazz Rulez.

"You come here to learn," Mr. Hanzen says. "And I do not play. You will be seated and ready to work before the tardy bell rings. You will raise your hand to speak or leave your seat. You will do all your homework and study hard for every test."

I don't like his rules.

I don't like his class.

And I don't like him.

"The other thing I want you to know, is that I do not call on volunteers," he says. "I will

2

call on you at random from this name jar."

He holds up a clear plastic jar with little cards inside. He shakes it and smiles like it's the greatest thing in the world.

"Each of you has a card in here with your name on it," he says. "You will not raise your hands. I will pick cards and call on you."

This is bad. Sooner or later, he's going to call on me.

He clicks on his laptop and goes to the next PowerPoint.

"What you see now are the learning goals for this class," he says. "Read them to yourself. I will then use the name jar to call on you."

I look at the screen. The letterz twist and turn like they're dancing.

Mr. Hanzen picks a name card.
"Erica, could you begin?"

She reads the learning goal
perfectly.

Mr. Hanzen picks another card.
"Teresa, your turn."

She reads perfectly, too.

He calls on the next person,
the next, and the next.

Everyone is smart.

But if he calls on me, I won't
be able to read it.

I look at the clock. The bell
rings in one minute.

Mr. Hanzen picks another card.
"Collin, could you read?"

I say nothing. Maybe he will
call on someone else.

"Collin Quinn," he says.
"Could you read?"

I look at the screen hard and

hope for the letters to stop moving.

They don't.

I have to get out of this.

"Sorry," I say. "I don't have my glasses. They broke."

"That's okay," Mr. Hanzen says. "Come up here to the front."

He points to an empty seat.

There's nothing I can do.

I stand slowly and take a step.

The bell rings.

I'm saved.

Everyone gets up to leave.

I see the laptop in front of me.

Mr. Hanzen looks the other way.

I grab it, slip it under my jacket, and walk into the hall.

2 DO YOU THINK?

HALLWAY. It was a dumb move to take that laptop.

I have to get rid of it.

I step into the boys' bathroom, find a stall, and close the door.

I'm safe now. But I have to be smart.

I use tissue and wipe the laptop clean to get my fingerprints off.

Minutes pass. The bell rings.

I'm ready.

I open the stall door and peek out.

Nobody is here.

I drop the laptop in the trashcan and walk out of the bathroom like nothing happened.

SECOND PERIOD. I get to biology and knock on the door. I'm two minutes late.

Mr. Iverson opens the door in his white lab coat. "Collin, not a good start for the first day of school."

He points to a clipboard with the late sheet.

"You know what to do," he says. "Print your name. You will also have detention."

This is another class I didn't pass last year.

He probably thinks I care about getting detention.

But I don't.

I find a seat in the back and get ready to be bored.

LUNCH. I walk to the food court. Alex and Leon are already at our table.

Alex is short with blue hair that sticks out. Leon is tall with strong shoulders.

I sit across from them and take my sandwich out of my backpack.

"Where is it?" Alex asks me.

"What do you mean?"

"It's all over the school," Leon says. "People are saying you took Mr. Hansen's laptop."

I look hard at both of them.

"Why would I do that? Do you think I'm stupid?"

3 SAME THING

AFTER SCHOOL. I'm home. I open the front door and step inside.

Everything is quiet and peaceful.

That's not how it was last night when Mom and Dad were screaming at each other.

I go to my bedroom, flop on the bed, and look at the ceiling.

The arguing has been getting worse.

Darlene can't stand it either. But she's lucky.

Next year she'll be away at

college.

She'll be living in a dorm,
taking computer classes, and getting
straight A's.

Everything is good for her. She
has a real future.

Most of what I have for a future
is nothing.

DINNER. I leave my room and step
into the kitchen.

Mom stands at the stove cooking
pancakes. She looks tired from her
job at the hardware store.

Darlene stands by the sink in her
volleyball sweats.

"Collin, how was your day?" Mom
asks.

I know I shouldn't lie. But
there's no way I can tell her what
really happened.

"It was fine," I say. "My classes seem all right."

She reaches out and gives me a side hug.

"This is going to be a good year for you," she says. "I can feel it."

I wish I felt the same.

We sit down and begin eating.

Dad is late coming home again, so we have a peaceful dinner.

I wish it could always be this way.

LATER. I sit at the kitchen table working on a picture for art class.

I take my time to get the shading just right.

It's a drawing of my backpack filled with books.

I wish I could read them.

Mom comes in and gets a bottle of

vodka out of the cupboard.

This is what she does when Dad isn't home.

She pours it into a glass and takes a sip.

"Nice drawing," she says. "It looks just like the real thing."

"Thanks."

"What about your homework?" she asks.

"This is homework for my art class. Most of my other work is done."

I wish it was true.

I haven't even started my other work.

THIRTY MINUTES PASS. Dad still isn't home. He's probably still drinking with his friends.

I take out a piece of paper and

begin working on the essay for my
English class.

The teacher is Ms. Gulliver.
She's tough. But she's nice.

I have to write a whole page.
It's going to take forever.

Collin Quinn
Englizh 10
Ms. Gulliver

ABOUT ME

*Last yaer my gradez were afwul. But
this yaer thingz are goign to be
bettre.*

*Im goign to work hard and get
good gradez in evrey class.*

*Some poeple think Im lazey in
shcool. But Im not.*

It just takez me longre to do

thingz.

I remeber Ms. Rayburn. I had her in the foruth grade.

She took tieme with me. I laernd a lot in her clasz.

And there wasnt anybodeye saying mean thingz to me.

Afther that, I dont know what happned.

But I was alwaze in the back of the clasz. The taecherz didnt like me.

Thats why I hoepe this year will be betrer.

TEN O'CLOCK. I lie in bed. The house is quiet.

I'm scared about school tomorrow. I wish I hadn't taken that laptop.

The front door opens. Dad's home.

"Where were you?" Mom shouts. Her

words are slurred.

Dad yells back. "Don't worry about it." His words are slurred, too.

I hear his heavy footsteps on the floor.

Mom shouts. "Don't you walk away from me."

I cover my head with my pillow.

But it doesn't help.

It's the same thing that happened last night.

4 ANY OTHER

WEDNESDAY MORNING. Edison High School. I get a bad feeling as soon as I walk through the front gate.

It was stupid to take that laptop.

I walk to history and stay in the hall as long as I can.

Finally, I have to go in.

The other kids look at me like they know what I did.

I have to stay calm and act like everything is okay.

Mr. Hanzen comes to the front of

the classroom. "Open up your books to page four," he says. "This chapter is about early humans."

I look closely at Mr. Hanzen. He seems normal, like he doesn't know what I did.

That's good. It means that nobody snitched on me.

ENGLISH. I get to my seat just before the bell rings.

Ms. Gulliver comes to the front of the classroom.

She has frazzled gray hair and a kind look in her eyes.

She passes out some papers.

"This is an article from yesterday's newspaper," she says. "Read it to yourself. You will have four minutes. After that, you will sit with your elbow partner and

17

discuss it."

I look at the headline. It's something about a family living in a van. There's a picture showing a man and his wife with two young kids.

I try to read it. But the letterz twist and turn.

I take a break and look around the room. Everybody else reads it with no problem.

How can it be so easy for them?

Four minutes pass. I've only read a few lines.

"Slide your desk next to your elbow partner," Ms. Gulliver says. "Discuss the facts of the article and your opinions about it."

My elbow partner is Jenny. I've seen her around. But I don't know her.

"What do you think about the

article?" I ask.

"I feel sorry for the family," she says. "That van is their home."

"What do you think is going to happen to them?"

"I don't know," Jenny says. "They keep traveling to find work. But there is no work."

I ask her more questions. She tells me about everything in the article.

If Ms. Gulliver calls on me, I'll be ready.

ART. Period six. I find a seat and get ready for class to start.

It looks like I'm in the clear. Nothing has happened about the laptop.

We sit at tables placed in a circle around a display in the

center.

It's an old work boot with the laces untied.

Ms. Somoza stands next to the display.

"Begin drawing," she says. "Let me see what you can do."

Art is my favorite subject. I draw the outline first. Then I put in the details and begin shading.

The picture looks good. I wish my other classes could be like this.

There's a knock on the door. It's a blue slip. Ms. Somoza brings it to me.

It says to see Mr. Wiley in the deans' office.

I have to stay calm.

If I was really in trouble, he wouldn't have sent for me with a blue slip.

He would have sent security to get me.

DEANS' OFFICE. Mr. Wiley is a big man with arms that bulge under his sleeves. His eyes peer into me.

Officer Krebb, the school police officer, sits next to him.

"Collin, are you aware of any problems that happened in your classes yesterday?" Mr. Wiley asks.

I take a breath. "Like what?"

"It could have been anything," says Officer Krebb. "We're following up on a report that came in."

I do my best to look innocent. "I didn't see anything. Everything was fine."

"Thanks for coming in," Mr. Wiley says. "You've been a big help."

I'm glad when the bell rings.

I go to my locker, get my stuff,
and go out the front gate.

I wonder if Officer Krebb and Mr.
Wiley talked to any other kids.

5 OVER

THURSDAY MORNING. Darlene and I go out the front door and begin walking to school.

I didn't sleep at all last night.

I can't stop thinking about the laptop.

I feel like I'm going to explode.

WORLD HISTORY. I walk in the door. Everything seems normal.

Then I see it, Mr. Hanzen's laptop.

I go to my seat and make sure I

keep my face blank.

Maybe it's okay. Maybe they'll quit looking for me.

Mr. Hanzen comes to the front of the classroom. He clicks on the laptop. A PowerPoint shows on the screen.

"Take out your notebooks," he says. "Today will be more about early humans."

I open my notebook.

He begins talking.

I hear his words.

But all I can think about is the laptop.

MATH. Third period. Nothing more has happened since history.

Mr. Nadler comes to the front of the classroom. "Open up your books to page seventeen."

24

There's a knock on the door.

Mr. Wiley steps in. "Collin," he says. "Come with me."

DEANS' OFFICE. I sit across the desk from Mr. Wiley. Mr. Hanzen sits to his left.

I try to act calm.

Maybe I'm not in trouble.

Mr. Wiley starts. "Officer Krebb and I talked to every student in the classroom. Seven of them saw you take the laptop."

I'm caught.

I get a feeling like I might throw up.

"Am I going to jail?" I ask.

"You're lucky," Mr. Wiley says. "Mr. Hansen doesn't want to press charges."

I look at Mr. Hanzen. I thought

he would be mad. But he's not.

"Have you ever been in the system?" Mr. Hanzen asks me.

"No."

"My brother went through it," he says. "And I know what happens."

Mr. Wiley speaks up. "I also know what it's like when it's hard to read. Is that why you took the laptop, because you didn't want Mr. Hansen to call on you?"

I didn't expect this. They act like they want to help me.

"I'm going to put you on in-school suspension for three days," Mr. Wiley says. "Your parents will also have to come in for a conference. Just remember, you could be going to jail."

He fills out a slip and gives it to me.

"Take this to the guidance room,"
he says. "You'll begin doing your
in-school suspension now."

I walk to the guidance room.

I feel relieved.

It's over.

6　NOW THEY KNOW

GUIDANCE CLASSROOM. I give my slip to Ms. Ogden.

She points to a desk and gives me a folder with the work I have to do.

"You'll be in here all day, including lunch," she says. "Your first assignment is to write one page about why you got in trouble and how you plan to improve."

It's a lot to write. But I have to do it.

I begin.

Collin Quinn
In-Shcool Suzpenzoin
Mr. Wiley

Why I Got in Truobel

I adimt it. I took Mr. Hanzen's laptop. I was wrnog to do it.

Evreything abuot shcool is bad for me. I dont undrestanb the work. The taechrz don't lieke me. And my parnets get on my caze becuase I get bad graedz.

It's lieke beniq at the botom of a hoel, and you cant get out.

The taechrs act like its all my fualt becuase I'm not tryeing.

But I am tryeing. It just takez me lnoger to do evrthihng. I dont know why.

My sistre gets A's. She's the

HOME. I open the front door. The house is empty. Darlene is still at volleyball.

She's a star in sports and a star in school.

I wish I could be like her. But I've never been a star in anything.

The thing I hate most is when people think I'm lazy.

They don't know how hard it is for me just to read one page.

And I can't stand the way the other kids look at me, like I'm nothing.

TWO HOURS LATER. I sit in the living room playing Sky Chaser.

Darlene comes through the front

door. "Collin, you know the rule. What are you doing playing a video game?"

"Don't worry about it," I say.

"How come I didn't see you at lunch today?" she asks.

"It's a long story. I was in the guidance room."

"What happened?" she asks.

"Don't worry about it."

Sometimes, I can't stand her.

I get up and go to my room.

THIRTY MINUTES LATER. I lie on my bed playing Sky Chaser on my phone.

I wish I could stop what's going to happen.

The front door opens. It's Mom.

I turn off Sky Chaser and put my phone in my pocket.

I hear footsteps come down the

hall.

She knocks.

I pick up a book to act like I'm reading. "Come in."

Her face is red. Her eyes drill into me.

"I got two calls," she says. "One was from Mr. Wiley. The other was from Mr. Hansen."

There's nothing I can say, so I say nothing.

"Mr. Wiley told me you stole Mr. Hansen's computer," she says. "What was that about?"

"It was a joke. I knew they would find it and give it back to him."

"I also had a talk with Mr. Hansen," she says. "He thinks you have a reading problem. He said you stole the computer because you didn't want him to call on you to read out loud."

"I don't know why he thinks that. My reading is fine."

She looks at me like she doesn't believe any of it.

"We'll talk more when Dad gets home," she says. "It's only the first week of school. What are you thinking?"

I wish I knew.

AFTER DINNER. I sit at the kitchen table and pretend to do homework.

Mom and Dad come in and sit across from me.

"Time to talk," Mom says.

Dad's face is red. He looks like he's going to blow.

"You could have gone to jail," he says.

"I know."

"You told me it was a joke," Mom says. "What kind of a joke is it to steal a teacher's laptop and almost get arrested?"

Dad looks hard at me. "I also heard what Mr. Hansen said. Why does he think you have a reading problem?"

"I don't know."

Mom opens my history book and puts it in front of me. "Read this," she says.

"I can read," I say. "I'm telling you."

"Go ahead," she says.

I look at the page.

I can't figure out what the words are.

I look again.

The letterz turn upside down and backwards.

"Go ahead," Mom says.

I try to read.

But I can't.

All I can do is sit there.

Now they know.

7 GIVE IT

FRIDAY. I sit in the guidance room for in-school suspension.

I hate it. We have to do the regular work for our classes. Plus, there's no talking. And we have to stay in here during lunch.

We also have to write eight pages about how to do better in school.

I still have two more pages to go. It's taking me forever.

I finish my sandwich and get back to work.

Collin Quinn
In-School Suspensoin
Mr. Wiley

My Gaols After High Shcool

My mian gaol aftre high shcool is to just be doune with it.

I try to do good. But evrey time I tunr arouond, somthing bad hapens. Most of it is bad graeds.

I alzo get tierd of the way peopel look at me. And its not just the taechers. Its the kids.

Its like they think I'm stupd.

What kind of job wuold I like to get someday?

My dad sayz I shouold think abuot the miltary. He's a mastr sargaent in the armey. But I dont thnik its for me.

*My mom wokrs at a hardwaer stoer.
I dont think I wuold liek that,
ethier.*

*When it comez to a job, I wuold
liek to have a good one that payes a
lot of mony. I alzo want a job that
I liek.*

*The thing I liek the most is art.
I wish I cuold be an artst someday.*

I get to the bottom of the paper. I
look at the clock. A whole hour has
passed.

I know my paper has a lot of
mistakes. But it's as good as I can
make it.

I put it with my other pages and
give them all to Ms. Ogden.

She staples them together and
gives them back to me.

"Collin, take these to Mr.

Wiley," she says. "He'll tell you what happens next."

DEANS' OFFICE. I give Mr. Wiley my eight pages.

I watch as he reads them. It's hard to tell what he thinks.

Finally, he finishes.

"Collin, your spelling and handwriting need work," he says. "But you do a great job of explaining your ideas. I'm impressed."

It catches me off guard to hear him say that. I thought he was going to say it was terrible.

"I need to ask you something," he says. "How do you feel about your reading?"

"It's okay."

"I noticed from your writing that

you had a lot of reversals," he says. "Do the letters ever move around when you read?"

"Like how?"

"Have you ever heard of dyslexia?" he asks.

"No."

"It's something that makes it hard for people to read," he says. "I have it. And when I try to read, sometimes my brain turns the letters around."

I can't believe what he's saying. He's talking about the same thing I have.

"Ms. Gulliver came and talked to me," he says. "She's teaching a new class after school for students who need help with reading. She wants to put you in it."

I doubt it will help. But Mr.

Wiley is looking right at me. I
don't have a way to say no.
    "Okay," I say. "I'll give it a
try."

8 BELIEVE HER

AFTER SCHOOL. I go to the library and find the meeting room.

Ms. Gulliver is there.

I see Leon, too. He looks embarrassed to see me. I didn't know he had a reading problem.

There are also two girls and another guy. I've seen them around. But I don't know them.

"Welcome to the Library Club," Ms. Gulliver says. "You'll be working here to improve your reading skills. Much of it is about reading more. You'll be choosing your own books and reading a lot."

I don't know if this is going to help me. It's the same thing I've had before.

"You will also be working on your reading skills," she says. "There's a reading problem called dyslexia. It has nothing to do with how smart you are. It's where your brain mixes up the letters you are trying to read. I'll be able to help you with that, too."

It's the second time today that someone has spoken about dyslexia. I wonder if I have it.

We get up and go into the main part of the library.

There's a table by the front with action books.

The first book I see is about an

earthquake.

The cover shows a kid walking past a bunch of wrecked buildings. Some of them are burning.

The title is *I Survived the San Francisco Earthquake.* The author is Lauren Tarshis.

I look at the first few pages. The print is bigger than in regular books.

Maybe I can read it.

The next book I see shows a kid flying through the air on a skateboard.

The title is *Grind*. The author is Eric Walters.

This book also looks good. It has big print, too.

I find a table and sit down to look at the books.

I can read more of the words than

I normally can.

Ms. Gulliver comes out of the meeting room and motions to me. "Collin, your turn," she says.

I go into the meeting room and sit across from her.

"It looks like you picked some good books," she says. "Which one do you want to work on today?"

I show her the book about the earthquake.

"Looks good," she says. "Open up to the first chapter and read to yourself."

I begin reading. It's easier than our English book. But it's still hard. There are a lot of words I don't know.

"Put your finger where you are and stop," she says. "Think about what you just read. What's it about?"

"A kid was in a building when the ground started shaking. The floor was going up and down like ocean waves. A bunch of bricks started falling. He thought he was going to die."

"Very good," Ms. Gulliver says. "Can you read it out loud for me?"

I know I'm going to mess up. But at least no other kids are here.

I go back to the first page and begin. A lot of the words are hard.

"Let's look at some of the sentences," she says. "Watch this."

She prints the first sentence in big letters and asks me to read it again.

There's a word I miss.

"That word is ground," Ms. Gulliver says.

She prints it in big letters and helps me sound it out. The o-u-n part is hard because the letters run together.

I write it five times and sound out the letters as I write them.

She prints another sentence. I have trouble with a different word.

"That word is rumbled," Ms. Gulliver says.

She prints it. I sound it out. The m-b-l part is hard because I get the letters mixed up.

I write it five times and sound out the letters.

We do more words.

It takes a long time.

But I can tell I'm learning.

"Let's see your writing," Ms. Gulliver says. "Write a few sentences about something that has happened to you today."

It's hard. But I write.

Uasualy I go home aftre shcool. But toady is diferent. Im in a class in the Libreary.

"Do you remember what I said about dyslexia?" Ms. Gulliver asks.

"You said it's when you read and the letters get mixed up."

"That's right," she says. "About one in every five people have it. For many, it's mild. But for some, it's severe. I think that's why it's so hard for you to read."

She looks at my folder. It has a picture of a car.

"Did you draw that?" she asks.

"Yep."

"Have you always been good in

art?"

"Yep."

"It doesn't surprise me," she says. "People with dyslexia are often gifted in other areas. Have you ever had anyone help you with your reading?"

"Not like this. People have mostly just told me I need to work harder."

"Things are going to change for you," Ms. Gulliver says. "Your reading is going to get better."

From the way she says it, I believe her.

9 CHANGED TODAY

ONE WEEK LATER. After school. Mom and Dad walk with me into the Edison Library.

I try not to be nervous. I don't know what to expect.

Mom seems okay.

But I don't know about Dad. It seems like something is bothering him.

Ms. Gulliver is waiting when we get to the meeting room.

"Mr. and Ms. Quinn, have you ever heard of dyslexia?" she asks.

"Collin told us about it last week," Mom says.

"It's very common," Ms. Gulliver says. "It's when people get mixed up on letters that look similar. They might think the letter b is the letter d, or the letter g is the letter j. It has nothing to do with intelligence."

I glance sideways at Dad. His face is red. I don't think he wants to be here.

"What does that mean for Collin?" Mom asks.

"He's always going to be dyslexic," Ms. Gulliver says. "But he can learn to work around it. There are many famous people who have dyslexia."

"Like who?" Mom asks.

"The actor Tom Cruz and the

director Steven Spielberg have it,"
Ms. Gulliver says. "The Governor of
California is dyslexic. So is the
Mayor of New York. They all had
problems in school because of their
reading."

Dad stares down at the floor. His
fists are clenched. His jaw is
tight.

"The main thing to remember is
that people with dyslexia can still
achieve at high levels."

Ms. Gulliver smiles.

I feel hope.

But what's going on with Dad?

HOME. After dinner. I sit at the
kitchen table and work on my
reading.

I have to concentrate hard when I
look at the words.

But it's getting better.

Dad comes in and sits across from me. He's drinking coffee, not beer. He and Mom have been getting along tonight.

"I'm glad I got to meet Ms. Gulliver," he says. "The things she said about reading made sense. I'm sorry about what you've been going through. I want you to know I'm proud of what you are doing."

He looks me in the eye and reaches across the table to shake my hand.

During all my time in school, I've always felt like a disappointment to him, like he didn't want me.

Something has changed today.

10 CATCH UP

FRIDAY MORNING. Darlene and I go down the front steps and begin walking to school.

"You seem different today," she says. "It's like you're happy."

"Things are getting better," I say. "Now that I know I have dyslexia and what to do about it, I feel like I have a chance to be good in school."

We keep walking.

Ten minutes later, we reach Edison High School.

I used to hate going through the front gate.

Today, I feel fine about it.

WORLD HISTORY. The bell rings. Mr. Hanzen comes to the front of the classroom.

Something is different. He doesn't seem grouchy.

"Beginning today, I'm changing the way we do things," he says. "I'm not going to call on you to read out loud. Instead, I'm going to have you read silently. Then I'll call on you to explain what you have read."

The fear goes out of me.

I won't have to be scared about reading out loud.

"Open up your books to page 64," he says. "The work today is about India. Read it to yourself. I will then call on you to explain."

I begin reading.

I'm not scared.

I can concentrate on trying to understand it.

AFTER SCHOOL. Library. I'm reading in my book when Ms. Gulliver calls me into the meeting room.

"Collin, you've made a lot of progress," she says. "I want to show you some new things to help with your dyslexia."

She pulls out a book and opens to the first chapter.

"This is written in a special font," she says. "It's called Open Dyslexic. The letters are thicker at the bottom and shaped so they are clearer. I think it will be easier for you."

I begin reading. It's a lot easier. The letters don't twist and turn as much.

Next, she pulls out a laptop computer.

"I'm checking this out to you," she says. "It has a special browser extension with apps to help people with dyslexia."

She starts the computer and puts it in front of me. "This will help you," she says. "The app converts the text on websites into Open Dyslexic."

She gets on the website for our city newspaper, the *Conroy Courier*. All of the words appear in Open Dyslexic. They are a lot easier to read.

"Here's another one," she says. "This will help you improve your reading skills."

She gives me a set of headphones.
I look at the computer screen. The
app highlights the words and reads
them out loud. I'll be able to
improve a lot with this.

"The last thing I want to show
you is the app that converts speech
into text," she says. "You speak
into the microphone built into the
computer. The app types the words
for you."

She clicks on the extension. I
look at the screen and begin
talking. The computer types what I
say. It's like magic.

After all this time of being left
behind, I finally have a way to
catch up.

11 BUT I'M NOT

HOME. After dinner. I sit at the kitchen table reading the book I got from the library.

I'm almost to the last page.

It will be the first book I've ever read from start to finish.

I come to a word I don't know, whistling. It's confusing to read because the letters in the center mash together.

I write it in my notebook five times in big letters and sound them out as I write them.

I do the same for the next hard word, terrified.

It takes a long time. But it's worth it. I'm learning the words now.

Next, I get on School View to look at my grades.

I have an A in art and a B in physical education. The other grades are still D's.

They are hard to look at.

But I know they will get better.

I just have to keep working.

Mom comes into the kitchen and sits across from me.

"How's it going with the new computer?" she asks.

I show her the apps for dyslexia and how they help me.

She smiles. But I see tears in her eyes.

"I've been so scared for you,"
she says. "Finally, I can see that
things are getting better."

I thought I was stupid.

But not anymore.

I feel like I have a future now.

TEN-THIRTY. Kitchen. Everybody else
is in bed.

I check my history report and put
it into my backpack. It's typed and
ready.

I wrote it by speaking into the
computer.

It's the best report I've ever
done.

The front door opens. Dad walks
in.

He comes into the kitchen. I
smell alcohol on him.

It makes me sad. But there's

nothing I can do about it.

"Collin, I thought you would be asleep by now," he says.

"I just finished my homework. Do you want to see it?"

I open my backpack and show him my history report.

He looks at it. But I can tell he doesn't read it.

"Good job," he says.

I open my reading notebook and show him the words I wrote.

He glances at it and looks away.

"Good," he says.

Next, I pull out my laptop.

I show him the apps for dyslexia and explain what they do.

He looks at the laptop but doesn't touch it.

"Did it cost anything?" he asks.

"Nope," I say. "The school lent

it to me."

I wait for him to say more.

But there's nothing.

I should be used to it.

But I'm not.

12   HEAD DOWN

ONE WEEK LATER. World History. I walk into the room. Mr. Hanzen is gone. There's a sub.

She stands straight with a strict look on her face.

"My name is Ms. Pike," she says. "Mr. Hansen left me his lesson plans. We are going to follow them, and you are going to learn. If there's a problem, I will call your parents and give detention. I will also be leaving a note for Mr. Hansen to let him know everything that happens."

Everyone sits up straight. I feel her eyes when she looks at me.

"Open your books to page 76," she says. "This is more about India."

She pulls a card out of the name jar. "Alex, could you begin?"

Alex is smart. He reads from the book with no problem.

But Ms. Pike is using the name jar.

And she's calling on us to read out loud.

I get a sick feeling in my stomach.

What if she calls on me?

Ms. Pike pulls another card out of the name jar.

It's Thomas. He also reads with no problem.

She pulls another card.

It's Leon.

I can't see his face. But I can feel his fear.

"Can I pass?" he asks. "My throat is sore."

"I can hear you fine," Ms. Pike says. "Please begin."

Leon puts his head down.

Nothing happens.

Then he starts. "The first In... Indian Em... Empire was high... highly cen... central... centralized. The king div... divide... divided the empire into prov... provinces ruled by gov... govern... governors."

Someone laughs.

Leon sinks low into his chair.

LUNCH. Alex and Leon are already at our table when I get to the food court.

Leon says nothing. He looks like he's been crushed.

It was bad enough that he had to read.

But the kid who laughed made it twenty times worse.

LIBRARY. It's four o'clock, almost time to leave.

Ms. Gulliver calls us into the meeting room. She has a look on her face like something is wrong.

"You should all be proud of the efforts you are making," she says. "And you should all be proud of your improvements. But I know that things are not always going to go well for you. Sometimes there are going to be setbacks."

Leon looks down. I wonder if he

told her what happened in history today.

"You have to remember that the problem with your reading has nothing to do with how smart you are," she says. "The problem is caused by dyslexia and nothing else. No matter what, you have to keep trying. Don't ever let anybody pull you down and cause you to feel bad about yourself."

It sounds good.

But when I look at Leon, he still has his head down.

13 CHANCE NOW

HOME. I unlock the front door and step inside.

The quiet is nice. I can relax.

But it still bugs me about what happened to Leon today.

I go to the kitchen, open my backpack, and take out the laptop.

I put on the headphones, go to the history book on School View, and start the app that reads it out loud to me.

I'm learning now.

FIVE-THIRTY. Darlene comes through
the front door.

Usually, she goes straight to her
room.

It surprises me when she comes
into the kitchen and sits across
from me.

"Collin, it seems like things are
going better for you," she says.

"Like how?"

"You were happy about going to
school the other day," she says.
"And now, when I come home, you're
doing your homework instead of
playing a video game."

"Reading is always going to be
hard for me," I say. "But things at
school are getting better."

"Like how?" she asks.

"When I look at a page, the
letters move around and turn

70

backwards. It's never going to get better. But I'm learning how to deal with it. That's what I like about this computer. It has an app that highlights the words and reads them out loud to me."

I give her the headphones. She listens to the words as they are highlighted on the screen.

"This is great," she says.

"My reading is improving. It's also helping me on tests because I can learn the stuff better."

The tone of her voice surprises me. She's not talking down to me, like she normally does.

"Will your dyslexia go away if you keep working hard?" she asks.

"It will never go away," I say. "But there are a lot of benefits. People with dyslexia have a

different way of looking at things.
It can make them more creative."

"Maybe that's why you're so good in art," she says.

"I don't know. Maybe."

She leaves the kitchen. I go back to work.

When it comes to school, it's always going to take me two or three times longer to read and write everything.

But I have a chance now.

14 REAL REASON

WORLD HISTORY. I get to class and take my seat.

I'm glad Mr. Hanzen is back.

But Leon is gone. And he never misses school.

I look around the room and wonder who laughed at him yesterday.

ENGLISH. Ms. Gulliver comes to the front of the room. A man I've never seen before stands next to her.

"This is Mr. Upshaw, our new college counselor," she says. "He's here to talk about your plans after high school."

He's a short man with a tie and a mustache. He doesn't smile.

"I know you're only in the tenth grade," he says. "But I'm here to speak about your future after you graduate."

He stops and looks at each of us. Everybody sits up.

"Some people think college is the only way to be successful in life," he says. "It's one of the ways. But what it's really about, is gaining a career skill. It can be something you learn in a four-year college. It can also be from a community college or career training program."

He passes out some brochures for Jasper Community College.

"Take a look at these," he says. "Then I will call on you."

The brochure has pictures of people repairing computers, installing solar panels, and fixing air conditioners. All of the jobs pay lots of money.

"Figure out what you like to do in your spare time," Mr. Upshaw says. "Chances are, it's where you have a natural talent. After that, make up a list of careers that go along with it. If you can get into a career that uses your natural talents, you can go very far."

I look at Leon's empty chair.

It would have been good for him to hear this.

LIBRARY. Ms. Gulliver calls me into the meeting room. I show her my notebook with all the new words I've learned.

"Collin, good job," she says. "I can see you've been working hard."

"I remember what you told us," I say. "You said that reading will always take us two or three times longer. I put myself on a schedule. I get up an hour earlier every morning and study. I go to the library and study when I get to school. And when I get home, I study for at least two more hours. I made a chart to keep track of everything and taped it to the wall in our kitchen."

"That's great," Ms. Gulliver says. "It shows you're taking control of your life."

She looks me in the eye. It makes me want to work harder.

"By the way," she says. "Do you know what happened to Leon?"

"I tried to call him at lunch. He didn't answer."

FOUR-THIRTY. I'm on the way home. I stop and knock on the door of Leon's house.

Nobody answers.

I call him on his cell phone. There's still no answer.

I leave a message and turn to walk home.

I wonder where he is.

HOME. After dinner. I still have more homework to do. My phone buzzes. It's Leon.

"How come you didn't come to school today?" I ask.

"I'm done with school," he says.

"I turned eighteen over the weekend.
I got a job working for a landscape
company."

"What do you do?"

"We dig up lawns and put in
plants that don't need as much
water."

"How much do you get?"

"Minimum wage," he says. "But at
least I'm out of school. I'm going
to pay rent and keep living at
home."

He doesn't say it. But I think
the real reason why he quit is
because of the kid who laughed at
him.

15 WHY DO I?

MONDAY MORNING. I sit across from Alex in the food court. It's almost time for school to start.

"It seems strange without Leon here," he says. "I didn't realize that school was going so bad for him."

"It surprised me too," I say. "I had no idea he was almost eighteen."

"He probably didn't want us to know, since he was taking tenth-grade classes," Alex says. "Did he say much when you talked to him?"

"He sounded like he was glad about working. But I think he just couldn't stand school any longer."

"I know it bugged him when he got called on by that sub," Alex says. "I could see it all over his face."

The bell rings. We begin walking to history.

It doesn't seem right without Leon here.

But in some ways, I'm glad for him.

Nobody will be calling on him to read anymore.

WORLD HISTORY. Mr. Hanzen is gone. It's that same sub again, Ms. Pike.

I can't stand to look at her after what she did to Leon.

She comes to the front of the room and gives us her strict look.

"Today we're going to begin work on China," she says. "Open up your books to page 84."

I open my book. The letters move around and change shapes. It's always worse when I'm nervous.

Ms. Pike picks a card out of the name jar. "Yesenia, could you start?"

Yesenia begins reading. It's perfect.

My face starts to sweat.

Ms. Pike calls on Robert. After that, she calls on Max.

It wouldn't be like this if Mr. Hanzen was here. He wouldn't be calling on us to read out loud.

"Continue reading on your own to page 87," Ms. Pike says. "The homework will be the questions on page 88."

It's safe now. I can breathe.

"One last thing," Ms. Pike says. "Mr. Hansen wanted you to know about the test this Thursday."

She pulls a card out of the name jar. "Collin, could you read what it says on the board?"

I look at the letters. They seem like they're dancing. I can't read any of it.

I act like I didn't hear her. Maybe she'll call on someone else.

"Collin Quinn," she says. "Could you please read?"

Everybody looks at me.

I stare harder at the board. The letters keep dancing.

I blink my eyes and try again. It doesn't help.

I hear laughing.

I stand up slowly and give Ms.

Pike a dirty look to make sure she knows I hate her.

I leave the room and walk down the hall.

I know I'm going to get in trouble.

But I can't take it anymore.

SIXTH PERIOD. I work on a picture in art class. It feels good to draw.

There's a knock on the door. It's Mr. Wiley.

He motions for me to come into the hall.

"What happened?" he asks.

"That lady in Mr. Hanzen's class called on me to read. I tried, but I couldn't do it."

"Where did you go?"

"Behind the food court."

"I know how you feel," Mr. Wiley

says. "And I'll talk to her. But
you're going to have three days of
detention for ditching class. You'll
start tomorrow at lunch. I'll also
be calling your parents."

He says he knows how I feel.
But he doesn't know.
Why do I even try?

16 FEEL CLOSE

TUESDAY AFTERNOON. The bell rings.
School is out. I'm sick of this
place.

I leave art class and walk to the
end of the hallway.

Normally, I turn right and go to
the library.

But I turn left instead and go
out the front gate.

Forget the Library Club. I'm
going home.

People tell me to keep working
hard. They say I shouldn't let the

dyslexia get me down.

But they don't know what it's
like.

I wish I was eighteen.

I would quit school, get a job,
and never look back.

HOME. I unlock the front door and
step inside.

The house is empty.

I sit back on the couch and start
Sky Chaser.

Maybe it will get my mind off
things.

TWO HOURS PASS. I'm still sitting on
the couch playing Sky Chaser.

The front door opens. Darlene
walks in.

"Collin, what's wrong?" she asks.
"I thought you were on a study

schedule."

I look away and turn up the volume. "Don't worry about it."

I'm glad when she goes to her room.

I'm sick of her.

I go to the kitchen and tear my study schedule off the wall.

LATER. I lie on my bed with the door closed.

Mom gets home.

I know Mr. Wiley has called her.

I wait for her to knock on my door.

Nothing happens.

A few minutes pass. Dad gets home.

He doesn't knock, either.

I guess they gave up on me.

DINNER. We sit down to eat.

Mom made chicken and rice, one of my favorites.

But I don't even taste it.

ALL I can think about is that I can't take school anymore.

We finish eating. Darlene goes to her room.

I sit alone at the table with Mom and Dad.

"Mom got calls from Mr. Wiley and Ms. Gulliver," Dad says. "Do you want to tell us what happened?"

He's asking me. But I know I don't have a choice.

I explain how Mr. Hanzen was gone, how the sub called on me to read out loud, and how I walked out.

I also explain how I didn't go to the Library Club.

A tear falls down Mom's cheek.

Dad leans forward. His eyes bore into me.

"Collin," he says. "You probably got your dyslexia from me."

I feel shock. I look at Mom and see the shock in her eyes, too.

"Reading has always been hard for me," Dad says. "The letters move around and change shapes. When it comes to words, I never know for sure what I'm seeing."

His voice is strong. His eyes stay glued to me.

"School was terrible. I was in constant fear that people would find out about my reading problem. I learned to cover it up."

I look into his eyes. I know the pain he feels.

"Don't be like me," he says. "You have to stand up and keep fighting."

He comes around the table.

He hugs me with all his strength.

I have always wanted this.

I feel close to him.

17 IF THEY CAN

WEDNESDAY. After dinner. A lot has happened since yesterday. Things are going better now.

I finish my new study schedule and tape it to the wall. Tonight will be my first checkmark.

Next, I get on my laptop to study for the history test tomorrow.

I go to School View, put on my headphones, and begin reading the chapter on China again.

I use the dyslexia app to read it in Open Dyslexic and listen to it at the same time.

When I'm done, I write down the main ideas.

It's slow. And my spelling is bad.

But I'm doing it.

TEN O'CLOCK. I sit at the kitchen table. The house is quiet.

I go back to the chapter on China to study more for the history test.

Mom comes into the kitchen and sits across from me.

"Collin, how many times have you read it?" she asks.

"Six."

"Do you think you know it?"

"I know it perfectly. But I don't want to take any chances."

"What about your spelling for the essay section?" she asks.

"Mr. Hansen said I can spell the words any way I want. The only thing that matters is what I say, not how I spell it."

She leaves.

I decide to do one more thing.

I get on YouTube and watch the video again about the Governor of California. He talks about his dyslexia and how he works extra hard to prepare for his speeches.

He has to practice over and over and read everything five times.

It's a lot. But he keeps going and puts in the work.

Next, I watch a video about the Mayor of New York. He talks about his dyslexia, too.

The other kids called him dumb when he was in school. He didn't know what was wrong with him.

But he kept going and didn't give up.

If they can do it, I can do it too.

18 I WAS

MY ALARM GOES OFF. It's five in the morning.

I feel like going back to sleep. But I get up, get dressed, and go out to the kitchen.

My laptop is still on the table. I put on my headphones, go to the chapter on China, and begin reading.

I remember everything. It's burned into my brain.

WORLD HISTORY. The bell rings to begin class. Mr. Hansen comes to the front of the classroom.

"There are fifteen multiple-choice questions and two essay questions," he says. "The test is printed in a special font, Open Dyslexic. It's easier to read for people who have dyslexia."

He passes out the tests. I begin working. The letters don't twist and turn as much as they normally do.

The multiple-choice questions are easy because I studied hard.

The essay questions are easy because I don't have to worry about spelling.

It has taken a long time. But I'm finally starting to feel better about things.

AFTER SCHOOL. Home. I'm studying in the kitchen when my phone buzzes.

It's Leon.

"Collin," he says. "I wanted to let you know. I'm coming back to school tomorrow."

"What happened?"

"The boss has been getting on my case," Leon says. "I also started thinking about things."

"Like what?"

"There's this guy who's been working there for a long time," Leon says. "He must be thirty years old. He told me he failed a lot of classes and dropped out of high school. At first, he thought it was great. But now, he has nothing. I don't want to be like him."

"What are you going to do?"

"I called the counseling office and talked to Ms. Boyle," he says. "She's going to put me back into my

classes. I'm also going to stop
caring what other people think about
me."

"What do you mean?"

"The final thing that made me
quit was when that kid in history
laughed at me. But I'm an adult now.
I'm not going to let other people
hold me back anymore."

I remember how I felt in history
when I got laughed at.

I was letting someone hold me
back, too.

19 FINALLY

WORLD HISTORY. The bell rings to begin class.

Mr. Hansen comes to the front of the room.

"I was pleased to see how you did on your tests yesterday, especially the essays," he says. "I'm going to read three of them. I'm not going to say who wrote them. But they are all excellent examples of being clear, concise, and complete."

He begins reading.

The first essay is about the

mountains and deserts along the
borders of China.

Everyone applauds when he
finishes.

The next essay is about farm life
in ancient China.

Everybody claps for that one,
too.

The final essay is about how
China was ruled by a series of
emperors.

I make sure I don't smile.

It's mine.

He finishes reading.

Everybody applauds.

I think about all the pain I've
been through in school.

I think about all the times I've
felt like a failure.

All of that is changing now.

Mr. Hansen said my essay was

excellent.

I never thought anything like that would ever happen to me.

AFTER DINNER. I start on my biology homework.

It's slow. But I'm understanding it better because my reading is getting better.

Dad comes into the kitchen. He puts a laptop on the table and sits across from me.

"Collin, I got this from the Army base," he says. "Do you think you could show me how to use those apps for dyslexia?"

I've always wanted this, a way to do something together with him.

He moves around next to me and opens the laptop.

I download the browser extension

for dyslexia and show him everything.

I watch as he goes to the website for the *Conway Courier*, clicks on an article, and listens through the headphones as the computer reads the words out loud to him.

His face lights up. I see a look of thanks in his eyes.

I think about all the times I've wanted him to be proud of me.

Finally, I know he is.

20 LETTERS

THREE MONTHS LATER. I enter World History. It's the first day of the spring semester.

I got a C or higher in everything on the fall report card, so I feel pretty good about things.

I find a seat near the front with Alex and Leon, pull out my laptop so I can take notes, and get ready for class to start.

Mr. Hansen comes to the front, looks at each of us, and clicks on his laptop.

A PowerPoint shows on the screen
that says Class Rules.

"For those of you who are new
this semester, you need to know that
I do not play," he says. "You will
be seated and ready to work before
the tardy bell rings. You will raise
your hand to speak or leave your
seat. You will do all your homework
and study hard for every test."

I look around the room. The new
people seem worried.

"The other thing you need to know
is that I do not call on
volunteers," Mr. Hansen says. "I
will call on you at random from my
name jar. It has cards inside with
each of your names."

I look around the room again. The
new people seem even more worried.

Mr. Hansen goes back to his

PowerPoint. "What you see are the learning goals for this semester. Read them to yourself. I will then call on you to explain them in your own words."

I look at the screen. The font is Open Dyslexic. The letters mostly stay still. I can read it.

"I will now start calling on you," Mr. Hansen says. "What is the first learning goal?"

He pulls a card out of his name jar. "Leon, could you explain?"

I remember when Leon hated to get called on. Not anymore.

"It's about the years between 1860 and 1900," he says. "You want us to know how the world changed."

"Nice job," Mr. Hansen says.

He reaches into his name jar and calls on another student to explain.

He then calls on another, another, and another.

"There is one last goal," Mr. Hansen says.

He doesn't pull a card out of the name jar. This time, he looks at me.

"Collin, could you explain?"

I take a breath. I want to make sure I say it right.

"It's about taking responsibility for your learning," I say. "It's about not giving up when things get hard. No matter what, you have to keep going and keep trying."

"Nice job," Mr. Hansen says. "That was very clear."

I think about everything I've gone through.

I feel proud.

The bell rings.

I put my laptop in my backpack

and walk into the hall.

It's crowded with everybody going to their classes.

I remember how I felt when the school year started.

I hated school and thought I was dumb.

But it's different now.

I know how to deal with my dyslexia.

I know I can learn.

And the letters don't get me down anymore.

ACKNOWLEDGMENTS

I would like to express my sincere appreciation to everyone who gave me feedback while I was writing this book.

COFFEE HOUSE WRITERS GROUP: Jenny Abrams, Noemi Arellano-Summer, Sandy Braccey, Susan Buckner, Osyris Chagoya, Nicholas Chiazza, James Cox, Dan Cragan, Nick Cruz, Paul Dandrea, Suzanne Fernald, John Goshorn, Lynne Horn, Steve Hovland, Julie Kim, Larry Kolk, Darian Lane, Bill Lanting, Donna Lee, Dan Levinsohn, Peggy Miley, Carson Mogk, Hope O'Connell, Miguel Quintero, Jared Reed, Karen Sexton, Chuck Su, AnneLise Wilhelmsen, and Ron Wolff.

SOCIETY OF CHILDREN'S BOOK WRITERS AND ILLUSTRATORS: Carlene Griffith, Kelly Powers, Jody Rizzotto, Kaitlyn Sanchez, Crystal Schreck, Suzanne Sutton, and Kathleen Troy.

FAMILY: Fahad Alomair, Waleed Alomair, and Betty Jean Thompson.

Thank you, Pam Sheppard, for your advice on creating this series.

Thank you, Laura Perkins, for your feedback and careful editing.

Thank you, Betty Jean, for your patience, your wisdom, and for being my wife.

ABOUT THE AUTHOR

My dream of becoming a writer started at Whitworth University. I was lucky to have a teacher, Dr. Tammy Reid, who believed in me and encouraged me. After college, I began a career as an educator, teaching reading and English at a middle school in Los Angeles. I went on to earn a doctorate in education. I also served as a high-school principal and district administrator. One of the most important things I have learned is that everyone can achieve success. Set your sights high, work hard, and strive to be the best that you can be.

FINDING FORWARD BOOKS

At Finding Forward Books, we publish easy-to-read novels with positive life lessons that show teens overcoming challenges in their lives. Our goal is to help young people improve their reading skills, develop positive attitudes, and increase their success in school.

The books are suitable for all students, including English learners and those with learning disabilities. Lexile measures range from 390 to 560.

The books have been praised in *Kirkus Reviews*, *Publishers Weekly BookLife Reviews*, *Foreword Clarion Reviews*, and *BlueInk Reviews*.

ADDITIONAL TITLES

TAKEN AWAY. A teen learns to cope after his dad is sent to prison.

NO PLACE TO HIDE. A struggling student improves his reading skills.

NEVER WANTED. A neglected teen is placed in a foster home.

ALL ALONE. A teen learns to cope with his mom's alcoholism.

KNOCKED DOWN. A football player learns the importance of honesty.

TORN. A student with everything learns to care about a student who has nothing.

OVERSPRAY. A teen experiences grief
after his father dies.

BLUE WALL. A troubled teen battles
back from depression.

CANS. A teen who dreams of attending
college struggles with poverty.

FINDING HOME. A homeless teen works
to build a better life for himself.

Finding Forward Books
Short Novels for Teens About
Issues Faced by Teens
www.findingforwardbooks.com